Thy Sacredshores

Words and Poetry

Norilen Anne V. De Jesus

Ukiyoto Publishing

All global publishing rights are held by

Ukiyoto Publishing

Published in 2023

Content Copyright © Norilen Anne V. De Jesus

ISBN 9789360496579

All rights reserved.
No part of this publication may be reproduced, transmitted, or stored in a retrieval system, in any form by any means, electronic, mechanical, photocopying, recording or otherwise, without the prior permission of the publisher.

The moral rights of the author have been asserted.

This book is sold subject to the condition that it shall not by way of trade or otherwise, be lent, resold, hired out or otherwise circulated, without the publisher's prior consent, in any form of binding or cover other than that in which it is published.

www.ukiyoto.com

For † CHLOE

My heart will forever reach for your paws

Contents

Solitude	1
Reaction	2
Eleanor	3
Stand Still	4
Blood	5
Clouded	6
Fallen Warrior	7
The Longing Poetess	8
Butterfly Kiss	9
Chaos	10
Shoreline	11
Dolly	12
Soul	13
The Vicious Cycle	14
Once	15
Rose-Colored Glass	16
Cold	17
Artificial Reality	18
Etched	19
Drowned	20
Free	21
Burn	22
Irony	23
1999	24

Angels	25
Hope	26
MCA	27
Surrender	28
Illusion	29
Wretched	30
Crowd	31
True Colors	32
Across The Road	33
Hearts	34
Nothing	35
Denial	36
Blind	37
Mother	38
Detached	39
Be Still	40
Tragic Truth	41
You	42
Lullabies	43
Inescapable	44
Radio Silence	45
Moment	46
Recoil	47
Prayer	48
About the Author	*49*

Solitude

Some days, we seek sunshine,
we immerse ourselves in sunlight
and roll around under
its enormous warmth.

Other days we seek darkness,
we cloak ourselves in gloominess
and spin around
its blinding nothingness.

'Cause sometimes,
it is only in the proverbial
black pit hole of despair
that we find solitude.

Reaction

She sat in silence
with emotions so raw
it digs deep unto her veins.

She stood in protest
with courage so immense
it cuts straight through her flesh.

Eleanor

Somewhere in this scorching heat
is a shelter of safety.
Somewhere in this stone cold earth
is a mantle of warmth.

Somewhere in this disruptive blare
is an oasis of silence.
And somewhere in this exhausting war
is a sanctuary of peace.

You are my refuge of comfort,
constant and deep,
an endless fountain of love,
grace and strength.

Stand Still

Once in a while,
the universe heeds us.

Once in a while,
fate turns life around for us.

And every once in a while,
we come back to life.

Blood

I will choose her.

I will choose her over my own pain,
my own hurt, my own anger
and frustrations.

I will choose her over my own pride,
--- and what's left of it.

Clouded

Sometimes, we think
we have lost things
but have not.

We think that
people are gone
when they aren't.

Sometimes, we are clouded
by the things we desire,
the unfamiliar emotions.

And sometimes,
we are wrong.

Fallen Warrior

To you, I hear you.
I have heard your thousand cries.
I heard your silent screams and every sigh.
And then I saw you, falling.

But in every downfall, in every defeat.
I see you fight, I see you rise.
I heard you, I saw you and I felt you,
so deeply, so intensely.

I touched you wounds,
they cut so deeply unto your every fiber.
I felt your scars,
they are marked so intensely unto your very flesh.

I turned to myself
and felt that same scar,
bled that same wound.
It stunned me, for I am your fellow warrior.
Fallen.

The Longing Poetess

I write every day and still miss writing,
I miss all the beautiful emotions,
the callous pain and the tragic truth.

I miss playing with words,
where words are my rhythm
and letters are my heartbeat.

Butterfly Kiss

As enchanting as when
a butterfly lands on a rose,
my butterfly lips
will plant you a kiss
without an ounce of
selfishness in it.

Chaos

For every glance,

I wish you could hear the words.

For every stare,

I wish you could feel the touch.

For every unspoken word

is a night that hasn't seen the day.

For every unfelt touch,

is a day that hasn't lived the night.

Unspoken words continue

to haunt us.

Unlived lives persist

to torment us.

Shoreline

I sit at the edge of the shore,
feeling the numbness
of my feet.

I stood at the center of the coast,
numbing the burning
of my hands.

Dolly

A pure spirit,
bounded by the
limiting walls of reality.

A beautiful soul,
freed in the
comforting hands of eternity.

Soul

Lying in a fetal position
at the bottom of
a cold, dark cave

The echoing sound
of raindrops
across the biting cold

And the spiraling dust
of nothingness
has brought shivers

to my aging soul.

The Vicious Cycle

Standing at the end of the tunnel,
I took two steps forward,
three steps back.
I took the same steps
for four more times.

I turned my back
then moved around,
turned around
and then moved back.

I kept going, doing
the exact same thing.
I felt numb, repeating
the same exact thing.

I looked around,
rotating clockwise
as I watched from the ground
and found myself
lying at the end of the tunnel.

Once

I saw you, twice
and held you, once.

I had you, twice
and loved you once.

Rose-Colored Glass

I looked closely through
the window of blinding lights,
stared intently into
a shadow of broken images.

Fragments of the past
continue to haunt.
Pieces of the present
ceased to propel.

Cold

I looked at you
with eyes, as warm
as a sunny day.

You stared right back
with eyes, as cold
as the winter snow.

It left me shivering
in the cold, frozen
through the night.

Artificial Reality

You saw me as your existent universe,
an absolute confession of truth.

But all I was is a false macrocosm,
a disorderly system of pretense.

Etched

I have never written about
anyone in my life, but you.
And have never allowed
anyone to occupy my thoughts, but you.

I have loved you far more than
I could ever allow.
And have etched you in my soul
deeper than I could ever escape.

Drowned

Inexplicably drawn to you,

I am.

Inexplicably drowned in you,

I am.

Free

Sometimes, in confusion
we find clarity.

And in clarity,
we find freedom.

Burn

There's fire
where it burns.

There's desire
and we burn.

Irony

How is it possible
to like
the same things,
but not want
the same thing?

How is it possible
to live
the same lives,
but not have
the same life?

1999

It was a brief moment
forever embedded
in my vulnerable mind

It was a lasting instant
eternally rooted
in my longing soul

In that fateful day in 1999
you left but remained
profoundly and infinitely.

Angels

Some people are angels
in disguise and
we don't know it.

Some people are angels
in our lives and
they don't know it.

Hope

The lights may dim,
but you
will not flicker.

The stars may fall,
but you
will not falter.

MCA

Melancholy has taken the city
into a deep slumber
Callous scars of the past caused havoc
to their kindred spirits

Awakened by the faint sound
of fluttering wings
Beams of light streaked across
the city skies

Vibrant colors of hope
splashed across the city streets
Compassionate cheers
marked the birth of a progressive era

Surrender

I'm alive but inside,
I'm dead.
I died,
a long,
long time
ago.

The battle has
long been over,
I have been defeated
a long,
long time
ago.

Illusion

I will come to you when you feel alone
I will come to you when you feel restless
I will come to you in your sleep

But do not search for me when you awake
Do not yearn for me in your waking hours
You will not find me.

Wretched

She is drowned with the love
she is willing to give.

He is drowned by the love
he isn't willing to take.

Crowd

Ocean of faces,
different people,
different struggles.

Have you ever wondered,
what is it like
to live their lives?

True Colors

I painted a picture of you in my head,
so delicate, so pristine.
I created an image of your spirit,
full of beauty and wonder.

The colors I painted you with faded,
so pale, so different.
You carved an image of your soul,
full of lies and deceit.

Across The Road

I watched as you walked past, slowly.
And I remembered the goodness in you,
the pureness of you heart.
I was reminded of all things
sweet and gentle
because that is who you are.

I witnessed your every step, intently.
And I knew the farther you are,
the further you have gone.
It was a revelation of all things
scarred but strong
because that is what you are.

Hearts

You are not invisible.
As delicate as you are,
you are seen by eyes that love.

You are not invincible.
As fragile as you are,
you are broken by hearts that fear.

Nothing

Nothing's right,
nothing's fine.
We hold on anyway.

Nothing's left,
nothing's changed.
We move on anyway.

Denial

Sometimes, we think
that the Universe speaks to us,
subtly sending us messages
we needed to know.

But sometimes, we realize
it is our hearts that speak to us,
softly whispering things
we already know.

Blind

You are not the one
in the eyes of the blind.

You can't be the one
in the hands of the callous.

Mother

You gave me a smile
your joy, you have given

You gave me strength
your spirit, you have given

You gave me life
your life, you have given

Detached

It comes like a thief in the night,
silent, swift and impactful.

It leaves like a thunder in the dark,
sudden, vicious and terrifying.

Be Still

Keep silent
and
the angels
will hear
you.

Keep still
and
the universe
will come
to you.

Keep your spirits high
and
the Lord
will rescue
you.

Tragic Truth

She was lost
in the madness
of his blinding illusion.

She was awaken
by the calmness
of the pressing reality.

You

You may not be the man of my dreams,
but you are the man in my dreams.

I may not be the woman from your vision,
but I am the woman of your fate.

Lullabies

You saw me from afar,
soaked and barely breathing.
On board a floating
wooden plank,
I lay.

I saw you from afar,
cloaked in your mystical hair.
On top of a roughly
molded rock,
you sat.

You swam across,
gently with shimmering scales.
I'll be your mermaid
and whisper you
soft lullabies,
you said.

Inescapable

I looked at you quietly
and watched endlessly.

You glanced at me briefly
and stared magically.

You and I are inexplicably
inescapable.

Radio Silence

It felt like a slow beat of the drum,
a throbbing pain in my chest
against the backdrop
of radio silence.

It felt like a sharp cut unto my skin,
an aching wound in my head
amidst the teardrops
of painful surrender.

Moment

In a moment of silence,
I knew we are one.

In that moment of intuition,
I knew you were the one.

Recoil

There is beauty in silence,
peaceful and warm.
There is strength in pain,
biting and deep.

And there is darkness
when the space between
the silence and the hurt
is an unforgiving inconvenience.

Prayer

I tilled the soil, until my knees were weak
I watered the plants, until the river dried
I poured my all, until I bled dry.

I waited for sunshine, until there was light
I summoned for rain, until it was in sight
I prayed for hope, until it was all that's left.

About the Author

Norilen Anne V. de Jesus

Norilen Anne V. de Jesus is a writer with a penchant for beautiful words and intricate phrases. She likes to play with words and uses poignant emotions in her writing. Her work is a journey of vast emotions, genuine and relatable.

She is a multiple university degree holder in the fields of Law, Communication and Public Administration. As her personal values command that she takes the high road, she occupies a small job as a humble public servant in her hometown.

www.ingramcontent.com/pod-product-compliance
Lightning Source LLC
LaVergne TN
LVHW041553070526
838199LV00046B/1942